DATE DUE

	JAN 25 2018		
NOV. 16 2004	SEP 19 2018		
SEP. 05 2005	SEP 21 2018		
SEP. 22 2005			
AUG. 31 2006			
JAN 30 2008			
MAR 19 2013			
SEP - 9 2013			
AUG 05 2016			
MAY 27 2017			

Vera's First Day of School

Vera Rosenberry

Henry Holt and Company • New York

Henry Holt and Company, LLC, *Publishers since 1866*
115 West 18th Street, New York, New York 10011
www.henryholt.com

Henry Holt is a registered trademark of Henry Holt and Company, LLC

Distributed in Canada by H. B. Fenn and Company Ltd.

Library of Congress Cataloging-in-Publication Data
Rosenberry, Vera.
Vera's first day of school / Vera Rosenberry. Summary: Vera cannot wait for the day when she starts school, but the first day does not go exactly as she has anticipated.
[1. First day of school—Fiction. 2. Schools—Fiction.] I. Title.
PZ7.R7155Ve 1999 [E]—dc21 98-43347

ISBN 0-8050-5936-9 (hardcover)
5 7 9 11 13 15 14 12 10 8 6
ISBN 0-8050-7269-1 (paperback)
1 3 5 7 9 10 8 6 4 2

First published in hardcover in 1999 by Henry Holt and Company
First Owlet paperback edition—2003
The artist used gouache on Lanaquarelle paper to create the illustrations for this book.
Printed in the United States of America on acid-free paper. ∞

This one is for Elaine.

Tomorrow was Vera's first day of school. She was big at last. Vera thought about her school. She had been to the playground many times with her sisters June and Elaine.

She liked the enormous buckeye tree.

She liked the creek she could see when she swung high on the swing set.

She liked to roller-skate all the way around the school on the smooth slate sidewalk, and fly kites in the grassy field.

The next morning Vera woke up early.
She quietly washed her face and put on her school dress.

Then she opened her book bag.
Everything was there.

Vera held her two big round pencils.
She smelled her new box of crayons.

In her slim black paint box,
the oval pans of colors shone
like jewels.

Since no one else was up yet, Vera watched the sunrise from her window and waited for the day to begin.

When Vera couldn't wait any longer, she flapped her arms in front of her sisters' beds and shouted,
"WAKE UP!
It's time for SCHOOL!"

After breakfast Mother handed the girls their lunches. June, Elaine, and Vera headed out the door to take a shortcut through their neighbors' backyard. Mr. and Mrs. Bailey spied them crossing a tiny corner of their perfect lawn.

"YOU GIRLS! Get off our property or we'll call the POLICE!" shrieked Mrs. Bailey.
"Run for your lives!" June yelled to Elaine and Vera.

When they made it around the corner, Vera pulled up her socks and straightened her dress.

She hurried ahead of her sisters. School was just a block away.

But suddenly Vera stopped. In the distance, she could see the school yard. It was full of children—more children than she had ever seen before.

Elaine and June ran off to meet their friends. June called back to Vera, "Meet us by the buckeye tree after school."

Then Elaine shouted, "Have a great first day, Vera!"

Vera stood under the buckeye tree. She looked at the children in the crowded playground. The giant green doors of the school seemed far away.

Vera sat down on a root to think. She watched a fuzzy caterpillar slowly climb up the tree trunk.

rrringg!

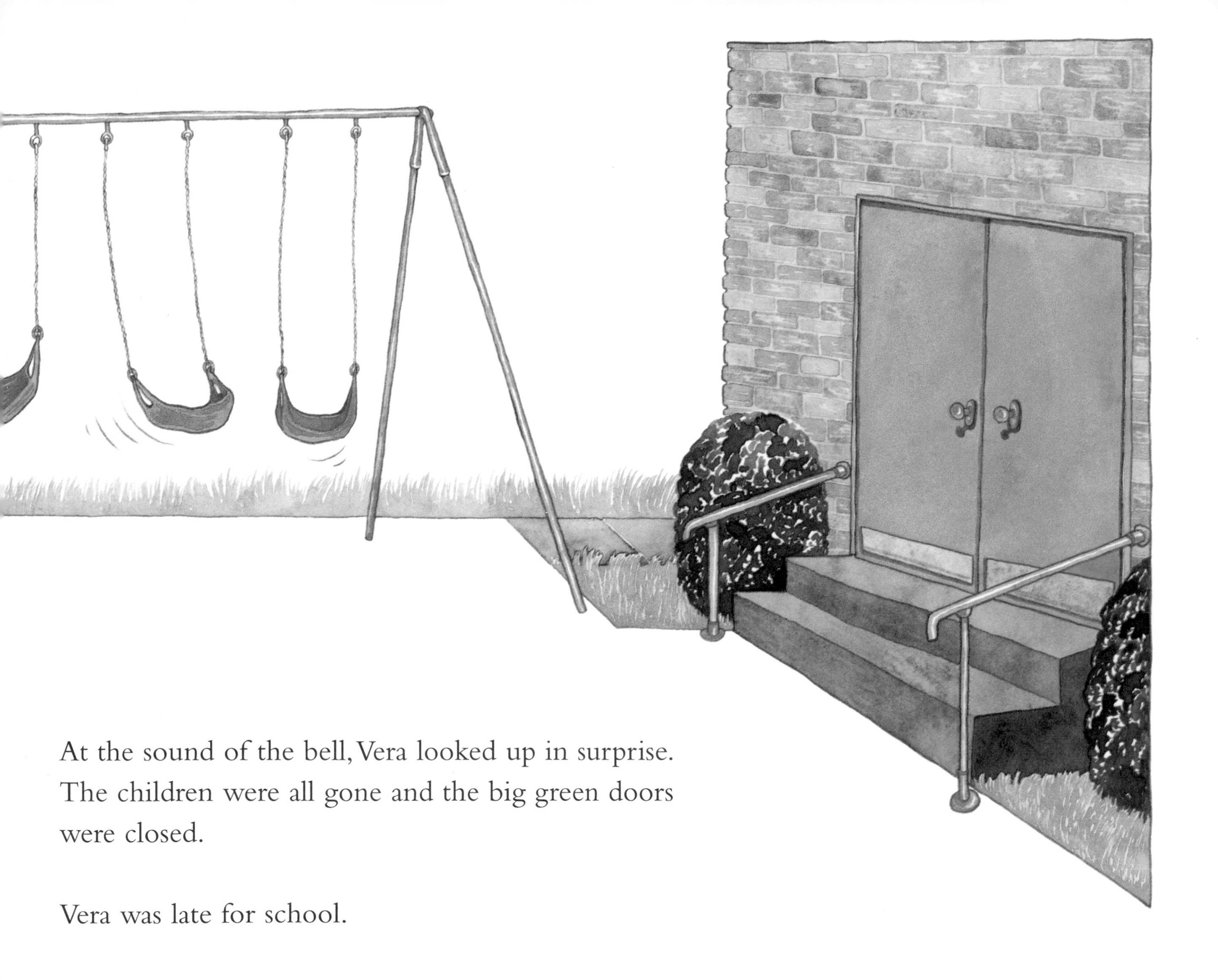

At the sound of the bell, Vera looked up in surprise. The children were all gone and the big green doors were closed.

Vera was late for school.

Vera didn't know what to do. Sad and lonely, she began to walk home. She took the long way so the Baileys wouldn't see her.

Mother was busy giving baby Ruthie a bath and didn't hear Vera come in. Vera quietly tiptoed upstairs to her room.

She crawled under her bed to think. All the other children were at school having fun. Big tears fell down Vera's cheeks.

A little while later Mother came in with the noisy vacuum cleaner.

She lifted the edge of the quilt to clean under Vera's bed.
"VERA! What are you doing here?"

Vera told her mother what had happened.
Her mother held her tightly.

Vera's dress was wrinkled. Tears had made brown lines down her face, and cobwebs were in her hair. Mother washed Vera's face and hands, smoothed her dress, and brushed her hair.

Then Mother put Ruthie in her buggy and they walked to Vera's school.

Mother opened the big green doors. She held Vera's hand when they came to Room 10. All the children were painting pictures.

"This is my daughter Vera," said Mother to the tall man inside. "She was not able to come to school this morning, but she is here now."

"I am happy to meet you, Vera. I am your teacher,
Mr. Kline. I was wondering where you were.

Here is your desk with your name card.
Here is a hook for your coat and a
cubbyhole for your lunch box.
Would you like to paint a picture today?"

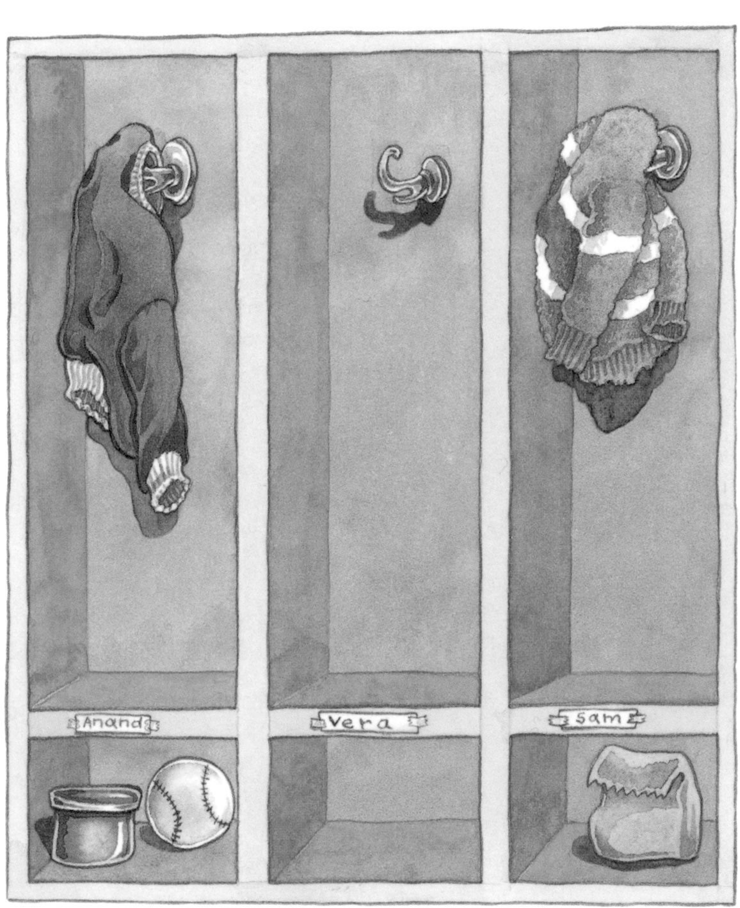

"Yes, please," Vera said.
She sat down at her desk and took her paint box out of her bag.

Mr. Kline gave her a large piece of manila paper and a small jar of water. A boy sitting next to her smiled in a friendly way.
Vera smiled back.

Vera painted a picture of the pretty flowers on Mr. Kline's desk.
She was where she was supposed to be—a big girl in school.
She was not afraid anymore.

At three o'clock Vera met June and Elaine by the buckeye tree.
"How did you like your first day of school?" Elaine asked.
"It was fun," Vera said. "But I think I will like the second day even better."

And she did.